A Junior Novelization

Adapted by Shannon Penney
Based on the original screenplay
by Elise Allen
Illustrations by Ulkutay Design Group
and Pat Pakula

SCHOLASTIC INC.

New York Toronto London Auckland
Sydney Mexico City New Delhi Hong Kong

ISBN 978-0-545-17766-5

Special thanks to Vicki Jaeger, Monica Okazaki, Kathleen Warner, Emily Kelly, Christine Chang, Tanya Mann, Rob Hudnut, Tiffany J. Shuttleworth, Walter P. Martishius, Luke Carroll, Lil Reichmann, Pam Prostarr, David Lee, Anita Lee, Andrea Schimpl, Tulin Ulkutay, and Ayse Ulkutay.

Published by Scholastic Inc.

12 11 10 9 8 7 6 5 4 3 2 1 10 11 12 13 14/0

Printed in the U.S.A. 40
First printing, March 2010

Chapter 1

Sunny, sandy Malibu has always been known for its pristine beaches, soaring canyons, and, of course, amazing surfing. And on the high school surf scene, no one was better than Merliah Summers.

At the latest competition, Merliah was feeling confident. As she paddled out into the water, she turned to glance back at the beach. Merliah could see her best friends, Fallon and Hadley, cheering and waving in the sunshine. Other surfers bobbed in the water nearby, waiting for the perfect wave.

But Merliah spotted it first.

It was going to be a monster wave, and it was all hers.

"Whoa!" the competition announcer cried back on the beach. "Will Merliah Summers really score that wave?"

Just then, the videophone-watch on her wrist beeped, and Fallon's face appeared on the little screen. "What do you think . . . will she?" she asked, grinning.

A wide smile spread across Merliah's face. "She will." With that, Merliah clicked off her phone and paddled toward the wave, angling to get into the perfect position.

And when a familiar song rang out over the announcer's speakers, she couldn't help grinning. It was the song Fallon and Hadley always played for her! She was going to win the competition with this wave, she just knew it. Like the song title said, she was Queen of the Waves!

She's the Queen of the Waves.
Check it out—she's spinnin' that board around.
She's the Queen of the Waves.
No one's gonna take away her crown.
(Her Majesty is dropping in.)
Surf's up! Bow down.
She's the Queen of the Waves!

As the massive wave reached her, Merliah took a deep breath, stood on her board, and skillfully dominated the wave.

"Merliah Summers drops in and carves it up!" the announcer cried in disbelief.

The grin on Merliah's face widened as the crowd roared. Merliah was never happier than when she was riding a giant wave.

But her happiness didn't last long.

The announcer spoke up again. "Whoa! Merliah Summers's hair is turning *pink*!"

What? Merliah reached up and pulled a piece of her hair forward. It was *bright* pink.

She glanced toward the beach. She could see the whole crowd staring and pointing. Even Fallon and Hadley were looking stunned.

"Check it out!" the announcer went on. "What is up with Merliah Summers?"

Merliah couldn't take it much longer. She shifted her weight to one foot. The board tilted and she dove into the water. She was swallowed up by the giant wave—it looked like a major wipeout!

Merliah was okay, though. She popped above the water and briefly waved to the

crowd. She didn't want them to worry, but she didn't want to face anyone until she'd figured out what was happening!

She swam farther under the water. There, she pulled her hair in front of her eyes again. It was still streaked with bright, shocking pink! Merliah shook her head and kept swimming away from the crowd. But before she could get very far, she felt something nudge her arm.

A dolphin!

But this wasn't just any dolphin. She was sparkly pink—and she was smiling.

"Merliah!"

Merliah looked around frantically. They were alone. Could the dolphin really have just said her name?

"Yes, I'm talking to you. Your friends are worried about you. Come. Hold on." The dolphin turned, and Merliah cautiously held her fin in her hand. Before she could change her mind, the dolphin took off through the water!

Water flew by them on all sides. Merliah couldn't help grinning. She'd spent her whole life in the water, but she'd never been for a swim like this!

After a few moments, the dolphin spoke again. "You do realize you're breathing underwater."

Shocked, Merliah gripped the dolphin's fin tightly with one hand. The other hand flew to her chest. Sure enough, she was breathing normally and they were fully under the water.

What was happening to her?

Before she could ask, the dolphin said, "We'll talk later." She nodded upward, where Fallon's and Hadley's familiar surfboards bobbed on the surface. Merliah let go of the dolphin's fin and popped up just next to her friends.

"Merliah! You're okay!" Hadley cried in relief. She didn't look twice at Merliah's crazy hair. It didn't faze her at all.

Fallon, on the other hand, couldn't stop staring at Merliah. Her eyes were wide. "Gnarly hair, dude. It's weird! Cool-weird."

"We found your surfboard, and not you, so we were worried! What happened out there?" Hadley asked.

Merliah sighed, steadying herself on her surfboard. "I don't know . . . but it gets weirder." She took a deep breath. Her friends were never going to believe this! "When I was underwater . . . it's crazy, but I was *breathing*. And a dolphin spoke to me."

Hadley listened intently. "Wow, there's something very deep and intense going on here," she said seriously.

Fallon rolled her eyes in disbelief. "Yes, like a deep, intense concussion."

"I'm fine," Merliah insisted. "Thanks so much for bringing my board back out. I really just want to go home. I'll call you later, okay?" And she paddled away.

Luckily, Merliah made it home without running into anyone who'd been at the surfing competition. Then she plopped down on her bed, thinking.

Merliah sat up as her grandfather, Break, came into the room. He smiled kindly at her. "Heard you ate it today. You all right?"

"Yeah, I'm good, Grandpa," Merliah assured him. She paused for a moment, then pulled back her hood, revealing her streaked pink hair.

Break grinned. "Hey! You dyed your hair."

"No, I didn't." Merliah shook her head, and her pink hair settled around her shoulders. "This just happened in the middle of the meet. Then I dove underwater, and I could breathe." She hesitated for a second. "And then a dolphin spoke to me." She lowered her eyes. "What's happening? Am I going crazy?"

Break sighed and put an arm around her. "No, you're not crazy," he said. "You just didn't know."

Merliah looked up quickly. "Know what?"

"I told you how you first came to me, right?" Break asked.

Merliah nodded. "Sure. It was after the accident when my parents died."

"It wasn't both your parents," Break said. He paused, deep in thought. "Your dad was always making up stories, ever since he was a kid. So when he told me he'd fallen in love with and married a mermaid, I thought it was just another whopper."

Merliah's eyebrows shot up, but she didn't interrupt.

"About a year after the accident, I was on the beach when your mom came to visit me," Break went on. "It was all real. Your mother was a beautiful mermaid named Calissa. She explained that you looked human, which made it dangerous for you to stay with her, and she asked me to look after you."

Merliah's head was spinning. This couldn't be real!

"Of course I said yes," Break added. "But before she left you with me, your mother gave you your shell necklace. Said it would always keep you safe." He studied Merliah carefully.

Merliah couldn't believe it.

She wouldn't.

"You really expect me to believe that my mother's a mermaid?!" Merliah climbed to her feet. Before Break could say anything else, she had stormed out of the room.

Chapter 2

A little while later, Merliah dangled her feet off a rocky outcropping over the water. Her pink hair waved in the ocean breeze. Fallon and Hadley sat next to her, listening as Merliah recounted Break's story.

"So I *am* losing my mind, because craziness clearly runs in my family, right?" Merliah finished.

"That doesn't explain your hair . . . but being half-mermaid might," Hadley said. She snagged Fallon's purple palmtop computer from her friend's pocket and started typing. After a minute, she pointed at the computer screen triumphantly. "This website says that in mythology, mermaids come of age around sixteen, and often go through physical changes—like longer or different-colored hair! That proves it!"

Fallon rolled her eyes. "Yeah, it proves that you can make up anything and put it on the Internet."

"It's not made up," Hadley insisted. "It's a real mermaid fact—and Merliah's proof!"

Merliah was truly exasperated. "I'm *not* a mermaid! I need help. I thought I was breathing underwater! I thought a dolphin was talking to me!"

Just then, a dolphin poked its head out of the water in the cove below them. "There's

a reason for that," she said. It was the same sparkly pink dolphin from earlier!

Fallon's jaw dropped. "This can't be happening," she mumbled in disbelief.

"No, silly, this is real!" Hadley cheered and turned to Merliah. "You didn't tell us she was pink and sparkly! Like diamonds and starlight. We should call her Diamond Starlight Dolphin!"

The dolphin laughed, then spoke again.

"Thank you! I do have a name, though: Zuma. I was very close with Merliah's mother."

"You knew my mother?" Merliah asked, curious in spite of herself.

Zuma's head bobbed up and down. "Everyone knew your mother. She was the queen of Oceana . . . until her jealous sister, Eris, overthrew her. Now Eris rules selfishly, putting Oceana in danger." She sighed heavily.

"So you're saying Merliah isn't just a mermaid . . . she's mermaid *royalty*?" Fallon asked.

Merliah looked at her always-practical friend in shock. "Tell me you're not starting to believe this!"

Fallon shrugged. "We're talking to a pink sparkly dolphin."

"A mer-princess," Hadley sighed. "That's so beautiful."

Merliah turned back to Zuma. "If all this happened years ago, why are you telling me now?"

"Because you've come of age," the dolphin said matter-of-factly. "Your mermaid self has resurfaced! Now you can come to Oceana and defeat Eris, just as the Destinies predicted."

"My destiny is to be the best surfer in Malibu!" Merliah cried. "Even if Oceana does exist—"

"Which it does," Hadley interjected.

"Why should I care if it's in trouble?" Merliah continued. "I don't care about any of this, including some make-believe mermaid mother and her make-believe protective necklace!" With that, Merliah tore off her shell necklace and hurled it against the rocks.

The magic necklace broke, but the pieces didn't scatter like Merliah expected. Instead there was an amazing flash, and glittery streaks swirled into the air. They formed an image of a beautiful but sad mermaid locked away in an underwater room. Three pink shells rotated in front of her, spinning under her magical control. Sparkly silver fibers flowed from the shells and floated in the water.

Zuma's eyes grew wide. "Calissa is still alive!" she cried gleefully. "I always knew it!" The dolphin splashed happily.

"I don't understand," Merliah said slowly. "This is my mother . . . right now?"

Zuma nodded. "Your necklace has that power because your mother filled it with Merillia, the life force of the sea."

Merliah looked back at the image of her mother. "Is she okay?" she asked quietly.

"No one in Oceana is okay," Zuma said solemnly. "Not while Eris rules. You're the only one who can stop her."

Merliah reached out toward the image. But before she could touch the image of her mother, it disappeared.

"I'll go down to Oceana," Merliah said suddenly, looking at Zuma with determination. "I'll help defeat Eris."

"And fulfill your mermaid destiny!" Hadley cheered.

"No," Merliah said, shaking her head. "If my mother can make a magic necklace, she can help me get back to normal. Then we forget any of this ever happened, and I can go back to my normal life."

"As you wish," Zuma said, and smiled.

Merliah took a deep breath and dove into the water. She grabbed hold of Zuma's fin and looked back up. "Please tell Break I'm okay," she called to her friends. "See you soon!"

"Good luck, Merliah!" they cried.

With a final wave, Merliah and Zuma plunged deep under the sea.

Chapter 3

Holding tightly to Zuma's fin, Merliah opened her eyes wide and watched the water stream by on all sides. She inhaled deeply—she really *could* breathe underwater!

It was a long journey, full of amazing sights. Zuma and Merliah swam through the night, but Merliah couldn't sleep. She didn't want to miss a moment of the beautiful underwater world!

By morning, they'd come upon the

outskirts of Oceana. Bright-colored coral ringed the city. Inside, Merliah could see homes, tall buildings, shops, and fashionable merpeople swimming to and fro. There was excitement and energy in the water. Merliah was itching to be a part of it!

"Is this Oceana? It's beautiful! Look at all the colors," she marveled.

Zuma sighed heavily. "They are beautiful . . . and terrible." She nodded to some glittery silver streaks in the water nearby.

"Is that what came out of my necklace charm?" Merliah asked. "Merillia?"

Zuma bobbed her head. "Yes, the life force of the sea. Only the royal family can spin it. Calissa's Merillia made the coral vibrant and healthy. Eris's Merillia isn't as

strong, so the unhealthy coral turns colors like autumn leaves."

Merliah studied the colorful coral. "So it's beautiful, but it's dying?"

"Exactly," Zuma confirmed. She winked at Merliah. "Now come—we need to get you a tail."

Merliah flinched. "A what?"

As Zuma headed into Oceana, Merliah

did her best to keep up. She stayed to the edge of pathways and ducked behind billboards, plants, and Zuma, careful to hide her legs. She couldn't help gazing around as they went, taking in the incredible sights around every corner. From the shops—Bloomingtails, Seaphora, and Fred Seagull—to the merpeople in fancy outfits toting pet fish, there was so much to see!

Merliah's tour was interrupted by a loud trumpetlike blast, coming from a funny-looking fish blowing into a conch shell nearby. As the sound rang through the water, all the merpeople snapped to attention. They poured out onto the streets, swimming quickly.

"What's going on?" Merliah asked.

"The Eris Festival," Zuma replied.

"We need to get you inside immediately. Hurry!"

Merliah grabbed Zuma's fin once again, tucked her legs to her chest, and let her dolphin friend tow her through the water. Zuma skirted the edges of the crowd and darted into a nearby clothing store just before another trumpet sounded.

Inside, Merliah let go of Zuma's fin.

Through the window, she could see crowds of merpeople lining the streets. They frantically cheered as a chariot came into view.

Atop the ornate chariot, which was pulled by giant jellyfish, rode a beautiful and haughty mermaid—Eris. Manta shark guards circled her, and a pufferazzi fish snapped her picture. The blue and green fish who had announced Eris's entrance with the conch shell now followed her, frantically tossing bright-colored anemones above him. They looked like fireworks!

"Oceana, do you adore me?" Eris called to the crowd. They clapped loudly. "Do you love me enough to deserve your Merillia?" Eris continued. The crowd cheered even more, trying to prove their devotion.

But Eris had spotted a large-lipped fish that hadn't been paying attention—she'd been too busy applying lipstick! Angered by the fish's lack of adoration, Eris spun her arm and magically created a dark whirlpool in the water. It carried the captive fish away to the dungeons.

"What was that?" Merliah cried.

Zuma was solemn. "That's one way Eris controls the merfolk. Her whirlpools are impossible to escape, as are her dungeons."

Merliah turned back to the window, frowning. She could see the shocked expressions on the faces of the merfolk lining the streets.

"Do you love me enough to deserve Merillia?" Eris asked again.

The terrified crowd broke into wild

applause, cheering at the tops of their lungs. Nodding with satisfaction, Eris leaned out and tossed Merillia into the sea, where it dissolved. Then her chariot moved off into the distance, toward the royal castle.

Merliah turned from the window, upset at the spectacle in the water below. She looked up at Zuma and said, "You said it's my destiny to defeat Eris. But how can I fight against *that*?"

Chapter 4

Zuma didn't have time to answer before the shop's front door swung open. Merliah quickly ducked behind a clothing rack to hide her legs. She watched in awe as two beautiful, energetic mermaids swam in, wearing fabulously fashionable outfits. They were followed by an adorable baby sea lion, who made a beeline straight for Zuma. The mermaids were thrilled to see their dolphin friend, too.

Zuma gestured back toward Merliah.

"Kayla! Xylie! I want to introduce —"

But Kayla cut her off. "Ooh, you need to see our new toy!" She zipped to a nearby wall, where a little fish happily waited with a dj setup. "It's a Deep-Sea-3 Player! Check it out!" She turned to the fish and he started to play. A bouncy, melodic song rang through the water!

"Let's dance!" Xylie cried. She and Kayla each grabbed one of Zuma's fins and spun with her in a circle, giggling. Snouts the sea lion joined in, swimming loops around the group.

Xylie spun under Zuma's fin. She leaned way back, dipping headfirst toward the floor—and came face-to-face with Merliah.

"Aaaaahhhh!" Xylie squealed. Startled, she lost her balance and went flying into the clothing rack. Everything toppled onto her—including Merliah!

Kayla and Snouts raced over, tugging at the clothing rack and trying to free Xylie. But before they could, Kayla spotted something unusual: Merliah's human toes!

"What are *these*?" she cried. "Xylie, look!"

Xylie and Snouts swam over for a closer look. But when Snouts got close to investigate, his whiskers tickled Merliah's feet!

"They're my toes," Merliah giggled, "and they're ticklish!"

"That's what I was trying to tell you!" Zuma told the mermaids. "I've brought a visitor—this is my friend Merliah."

"But . . . she's human!" Kayla blurted out.

"Half-human," Zuma corrected her.

"Her mother is Calissa. And we've seen proof that Calissa is alive."

Kayla and Xylie gasped.

"Then Merliah can fulfill the prediction! She's the princess—she can overthrow Eris!" Kayla said.

Xylie chimed in, "And Calissa can rule Oceana again!"

"But how?" Merliah asked her new friends. "Eris is so powerful. . . ."

"We'll help you!" Xylie added. Snouts barked his approval.

"We should see the Destinies!" Kayla added, nodding. "They'll know just what to do."

Zuma smiled widely, flicking her tail. "Before we leave, I'm hoping you can do something about . . ." She nodded toward Merliah's legs.

Kayla and Xylie squealed with glee. "Tail makeover!"

The Deep-Sea-3 Player sprang into action, and music filled the water. Xylie, Kayla, and Snouts pulled fashions, jewelry, and accessories from all around the store. In a whirl of excitement, they tried all sorts of cool outfit combinations around Merliah's legs. Finally, they created a fake tail that was a perfect fit. It was stunning!

Merliah couldn't help laughing. She swam across the store in her new tail, posing like a supermodel, while the mermaids cheered.

"What do you think?" Merliah asked, turning to Zuma.

The dolphin grinned. "Let's go see the Destinies."

Chapter 5

The three Destinies, Dee, Deanne, and Deandra, had the best salon in Oceana. Not only were they fabulous stylists, they had a knack for telling the future.

Shortly after the Eris Festival, the conch shell sounded in the Destinies' House of Fate salon. It was Remo, announcing the queen's entrance! Eris came to the salon every day to have her hair done and hear what the Destinies predicted for the fate of her kingdom, so her visit was no surprise.

Eris flung the door open with a crash, smushing Remo against the wall. "Destinies! Make me beautiful and tell me what I want to hear!"

The Destinies bustled around the salon and tended to Eris's hair. But before long, their tones turned serious and they began to glow softly, in various colors that matched their outfits. They were having visions!

"The Merillia is weak," Dee said gravely, speaking in a trance. "Without a change, you'll poison Oceana."

Eris sighed. "Yes, I know. I'm working on that."

Deanne shook her head, and the aura of light around her head moved, too. "You won't have time. Calissa's daughter has come of age."

Eris's head whipped around to look at

the Destinies in shock. This was the first time they hadn't told her exactly what she'd wanted to hear! "What? Calissa has no daughter!"

"There is a daughter . . . who can destroy you," Deandra noted.

Eris clutched the armrests of her chair. "Then I will destroy her first," she said darkly. "Where can I find her?"

But just as suddenly as it had started, the Destinies' vision came to an end. Their colorful auras vanished, and they toyed with Eris's hair as if nothing had happened.

Furious, Eris pushed them for more information. "Where is Calissa's daughter? What does she look like? I demand you answer me!"

Deanne giggled. "Eris, we're done. You

know that too much predicting gives us mega-headaches!"

Frustrated, Eris rose to her feet and stormed toward the foyer of the salon . . .

. . . where Merliah and her friends had just entered!

Xylie heard Eris's cry from the other side of the foyer door. The mermaids, Zuma, Snouts, and Merliah peered around frantically. A display of wigs on mannequin heads lined one wall, which gave Merliah an idea. Merliah quickly swam behind a beautiful sculpture to hide. She could only hope that Eris wouldn't spot her.

Meanwhile, the others met Eris at the foyer door to distract her. Remo was close behind his queen. "Eris, we were looking for you!" Xylie cried enthusiastically.

"We have some gorgeous new items in

the store that we wanted to show exclusively to you," Kayla added.

"Wait!" Eris cried. "You may be the first to hear my new edict." She cleared her throat. "I hereby declare that strangers or anyone suspicious must be turned in to me immediately!"

"I think I did see a stranger!" Kayla said quickly, trying to keep Eris from noticing Merliah.

Xylie jumped in. "We can point you in the right direction!"

With that, Xylie, Kayla, and Snouts led Eris and Remo out of the salon foyer—and safely away from Merliah.

For now.

Once the coast was clear, Merliah and Zuma swam into the main salon. When the Destinies spotted Merliah, they perked up.

"Great hair!" Deanne said, ushering Merliah to a chair.

Deandra agreed. "Love the pink!"

Merliah looked at Zuma, skeptical. "*These* are the Destinies?" she whispered. They weren't exactly what she'd expected!

Zuma nodded as Xylie, Kayla, and Snouts swam back into the salon.

"I think we distracted Eris for a little bit," Xylie said, flopping down in a chair.

Kayla nodded. "But not for long. She won't rest until she finds Calissa's daughter."

At those words, the three Destinies froze again. Their auras returned, glowing softly. They were having another vision!

"You are meant to overthrow Eris," Deanne said, in a trance, to a stunned Merliah. "But the three tools you need are spread far and wide."

Dee jumped in. "The Celestial Comb . . ."

". . . a dreamfish . . ." Deanne added.

Deandra finished the list. ". . . and Eris's own protective necklace."

Merliah looked to each of them with wide eyes. "If I get these things and defeat Eris, will I be normal again?"

Deanne replied. "You will get what you seek."

"But how?" Kayla burst out. "The Celestial Comb and the dreamfish don't

even exist!"

Zuma looked thoughtful. "I always thought they were myths . . . until now."

It all sounded awfully fishy to Merliah, but she was desperate to get her old life back. "How do we know you're for real?" she asked the Destinies.

"You don't," Dee answered simply.

And with that, the Destinies' auras

disappeared and the three mermaids were back to normal, oohing and aahing over Merliah's pink hair.

Merliah and her friends thanked the stylists and headed for the door, but Deanne called after them, "Tell Fallon she's going to be bumped up to the varsity surf team before the next meet!" She stopped and looked utterly confused for a minute as the glow around her faded, then she giggled. "I don't even know what that means!"

Merliah looked back at her, jaw hanging open. The Destinies weren't a hoax after all!

Chapter 6

As Zuma led the way out of the salon, the friends debated what to do next.

"Should we start with the Celestial Comb?" Zuma suggested.

Xylie shrugged. "There is no Celestial Comb—it's a myth!"

"Where I live, mermaids and talking dolphins are myths," Merliah said quietly. "What's the story about the Celestial Comb?"

Zuma told the story of an ancient hair

comb once worn by the queens of Oceana. It had been lost for hundreds of years. According to the story, only the true heir of Oceana could retrieve it from the place "where merfolk can see but never touch."

Kayla studied Merliah's thoughtful face. "Doesn't give us much to go on, does it?"

"No," Merliah said slowly. "But I think I know where we can find out more." She glanced down at the fancy videophone-watch on her wrist, which she used to communicate with her friends while surfing.

She dialed Fallon's number, and her friend picked up immediately. Hadley popped up just next to Fallon on the screen.

"Are you okay?" Fallon asked anxiously.

Merliah smiled. "I'm fine. I'm in Oceana."

Kayla and Xylie peered at the screen in awe, anxious to see more humans. "Do they have toes, too?" Kayla asked.

"Ten of 'em! Check it out!" Hadley cried, wiggling her toes at the screen and grinning. While Fallon stared at Merliah's real, live mermaid friends, Hadley took it all in stride.

"I need your help," Merliah went on.

"Can you search online for 'Celestial Comb'?"

Maybe Fallon couldn't quite believe that she was looking at mermaids, but she could research solid facts. She did a quick search on her computer, but came up with nothing.

Merliah thought for a moment. "Where could a place be that 'merfolk may see but never touch'?"

"We can't touch things on land," Xylie mused.

"Can't see them there, either," Kayla added.

Merliah was beginning to get an idea. She turned back to her wrist phone. "Fallon, are there any underwater caves off the California coast? Caves with big air pockets inside?"

Fallon typed away on her keyboard. "Yes! The Yafos Caves."

Zuma spun joyfully in the water. "I know where that is."

Merliah's face broke into a huge smile. "Thanks, Fallon! Hey, before you go, great news—Coach is going to bump you up to varsity before the next surf meet."

Fallon looked confused. "Did she tell you that?"

Merliah shook her head and smiled. "I just know." With that, she waved to her friends and hung up.

The journey to the caves was long. The coral outside Oceana was even brighter and more unhealthy. It made them all sleepy and sluggish! But that wasn't their only problem.

Once Merliah and her friends reached the caves, they spotted their biggest obstacle yet. The entrance to the caves was blocked by a huge group of giant, bright orange jellyfish . . . and they looked *mean*!

"Their sting is deadly, and they're very protective of their home," Zuma whispered.

Merliah hung back and studied the

scene. "How do we get the comb?"

The friends all paused, thinking hard.

Then Kayla straightened up, looking determined. "We can't—but you can. Snouts can help you." She turned to Xylie and Zuma. "If the jellyfish go after the rest of us, Merliah can get inside."

Merliah couldn't believe what her friends were planning to do. It was so dangerous! But it was their only chance to get the comb.

"Let's do it," she said.

Merliah and Snouts ducked behind a big chunk of coral, out of sight. Meanwhile, Kayla, Xylie, and Zuma swam directly toward the caves.

"Hey, jellies!" Kayla called. "Mind if we come in?"

In no time, the giant jellyfish were on the

chase! They darted after the mermaids and Zuma, who spun and ducked and swirled through the water to avoid them. Some of the jellyfish got tangled in one another's tentacles; others were hot on the mermaids' tails.

Merliah's moment had come! While the jellyfish were distracted, she and Snouts slipped into the cave. Inside, it was a long swim upward. But finally, they broke the surface of the water. The cave had a big air pocket inside!

Merliah studied the shimmering crystal walls of the cave. High up, a glint of gold caught her eye. She grinned at Snouts.

"The Celestial Comb—'where merfolk may see but never touch,'" she repeated. "Good thing I'm not merfolk."

Pulling up her fake tail fabric and tying

it off to the side, Merliah began climbing the rock. Snouts watched anxiously as she made her way slowly up the side of the cave, slipping and nearly falling. Finally, she reached the golden object. It *was* the Celestial Comb!

But when she pulled on it, the comb was firmly stuck in the rock. She tried again and again, but with no luck.

Below, Snouts barked encouragement. Glancing down at him, Merliah adjusted her feet. As she stepped on a stone jutting out of the wall near her right foot, it began to glow! Merliah's eyes widened. She pulled on the comb, and though it didn't come free, it did wiggle slightly in her hand. She was on the right track!

Merliah studied the rock around her more carefully, poking and prodding various stones with her free hand and foot. Before long, another stone began to glow, and the comb got even looser. When Merliah finally touched the third magical stone, the comb slid out easily into her other hand!

"I've got it!" Merliah cried down to Snouts. He clapped his fins and did a backflip.

Holding the comb tight in one hand, Merliah dove back into the water. Together, she and Snouts headed out to the entrance of the cave. But as they got closer, they could see that something wasn't right.

They heard a large *crack!* as pieces of crystal started to fall all around them. The falling rocks were about to block the entrance completely! Merliah and Snouts would be trapped.

The two friends picked up speed and

swam as fast as they could. With a burst of speed, they zoomed out of the cave just before the crystal rocks sealed off the entrance for good!

On the other side, they found Xylie, Kayla, and Zuma were thrilled to see that they were okay. "You made it!" Xylie cried.

"I have the comb," Merliah said excitedly, and the friends celebrated.

Chapter 7

Meanwhile, Eris and Remo searched all over Oceana for Merliah. But no one had seen her! Determined, Eris decided to seek answers from someone else—Calissa.

Eris stormed down to the depths of the castle, where Calissa was trapped in the dungeon. She flung open Calissa's cell door, glaring at her sister. Calissa was spinning thin strands of Merillia.

"I spoke with the Destinies today," Eris spat. "They gave me good news. I'm an aunt!"

Calissa stiffened as she tried to cover up what she knew. "What long-lost sibling is the lucky parent?"

Eris laughed mockingly. "Nice try, sis. You found a way to hide her from me a long time ago, but now she's all grown up, and here in Oceana." Her eyes narrowed. "Tell me how to find her."

Calissa sighed. "How would I know? Even if I did have a daughter, I've been locked up for fifteen years. I wouldn't know anything about her."

"Oh, but I'm sure you know what merman is her father!" Eris said, studying her sister's face. "Unless . . . is it that *human* you used to moon over?"

Calissa turned away and said, "I don't know what you're talking about."

Eris knew her sister well—and she could tell that she was lying. "A half-human? That's who's supposed to take over my throne?" She looked Calissa directly in the eyes. "Better give me a clue how to find her. Then maybe I'll show her some mercy."

Calissa remained silent.

"That's your decision." Eris shrugged. "But I'll find her. And until I do, every hour you don't tell me what I want to know, I will imprison ten of our innocent subjects." Her face turned hard and wicked. "Those merfolk will be placed in my dungeons forever!"

Calissa had nothing to say.

Eris turned to leave, but then faced her sister one last time. "The Merillia you're spinning is still terrible. You're poisoning Oceana."

"No, you are," Calissa answered firmly. "My Merillia reflects my emotions. It will only improve when you set me free."

Eris's fingers tightened on the cell door, but she stayed calm and turned to Remo. "Send out my manta sharks to find Calissa's daughter. We'll keep just a few behind . . . while I choose this hour's ten innocents." She smiled sweetly at Calissa. "Happy spinning, sis. Enjoy your guilt."

And with that, Eris disappeared, leaving Calissa alone in the dungeon.

Chapter 8

Soon the friends made their way to the open ocean.

But danger lurked nearby.

Zuma spotted Eris's manta sharks scanning the water above. The dolphin pulled everyone into hiding just in time.

"The Destinies said we have to find a dreamfish next," Merliah whispered as the manta sharks swam away. "What's that?"

Xylie piped up. "They're magical fish

that can never be captured. If you impress one and earn its loyalty, it will offer you your greatest desire. You can only call it once."

Merliah nodded. "In the stories, where do you find dreamfish?"

"The story says they live 'under the horse and the bear . . .' but I don't know what that means," Xylie explained.

Without hesitating, Merliah dialed her videophone-watch again.

Fallon answered, bursting with excitement. "Merliah! You were right—Coach bumped me up to varsity!"

Merliah smiled. The Destinies really *did* know what they were talking about!

"Congrats! I need anything you can find online about dreamfish who live 'under the horse and the bear,'" she said urgently.

Fallon typed away on her computer. "Nothing."

"Try this," Merliah said, her eyes lighting up. "Remember our class trip to Sedona, and all those rock formations that looked like dogs, or birds, or a coffeepot?"

"Above-water rock formations," Kayla said, understanding. "No wonder we'd never know where to find them."

"Got it!" Fallon cried a moment later. "'Rising from the middle of the Pacific Ocean's Andenato Current, the horse and the bear majestically face each other.'"

"I know the Andenato Current," Zuma said.

But Kayla put a hand on Zuma's side to silence her. As the group followed Kayla's gaze, they saw the manta sharks circling overhead again. This time, their beady red eyes were on Merliah and her friends.

"Gotta go," Merliah whispered into the phone. "Thanks."

"Swim!" Zuma directed. "Follow me!"

The friends took off after Zuma, swimming as fast as they could. The manta sharks were right behind them!

Before long, Merliah started to fall behind. Snouts tried to nudge her along, but with no luck. The lead manta shark was about to catch Merliah. . . .

But Zuma circled back just in time! Merliah clung to Zuma's fin as they raced through the water, dodging between rock formations and staying only a few strokes ahead of the manta sharks.

Finally, Zuma ducked into a thin opening that led to an underwater cavern. The others were right behind her as the manta sharks

slammed into the rock. The opening was too small for them . . . but that didn't stop them from bashing it open.

"They're going to get in!" Kayla cried.

Zuma led them to a narrow exit at the far end of the cavern, just as the manta sharks broke in from the other side. Before the manta sharks could see them, the friends swam in the other direction. Soon there was no sign of Merliah, Zuma, Snouts, or the mermaids anywhere.

After their narrow escape, Merliah and her friends followed Zuma's lead to the Andenato Current. The wide blue current cut through the water, looking impossibly fast and strong.

Kayla studied it from a distance. "How can we tell if the dreamfish are in there?"

Trying to help, Snouts dove into the current. But he shot back out again a second later, barking in surprise.

Zuma laughed. "The current is way too strong to swim inside," she noted.

Merliah's eyes lit up as she noticed a long, flat shell on the sand nearby. "Why swim when we can shred?" Tying her fake tail off to the side again, Merliah grabbed the shell

and paddled into the racing current!

As soon as she was inside, Merliah stood on the shell like a surfboard. She rode the current like a giant wave. All around her, Merliah could see colorful, pretty fish—dreamfish! They giggled and frolicked as she surfed the current. It was magical!

As Merliah shot back into the open water, her friends surrounded her. "Did you earn their loyalty?" Kayla asked.

Merliah glanced around hopefully, but no dreamfish had followed her. Her heart sank. "I guess not."

Just then, Snouts let out an urgent bark. They all turned to see a single dreamfish popping out of the current!

The young fish bobbed in front of Merliah's face. "Call me when you need me," he said. He quickly nuzzled her nose and zipped away again.

Kayla and Xylie squealed and squished Merliah in a massive hug.

"Now all we need to do is get Eris's necklace," Zuma noted.

"Maybe we could sneak into the castle and take it off her when she sleeps," Kayla suggested.

Zuma shook her head. "We could never get past the guards."

"When is the next Eris Festival?" Merliah asked suddenly.

"A few hours from now," Xylie said.

A slow smile came over Merliah's face. "I think I know how we can get close to Eris at the festival. We need the Deep-Sea-3 player and I just need to know one thing." She raised an eyebrow at her new friends. "Can you dance?"

Chapter 9

Back in Oceana, a huge crowd had gathered for the latest Eris Festival. Merliah and her friends were eager to put their plan into action. But their spirits fell as they noticed whirlpools off in the distance.

"Why are there so many whirlpools?" Merliah asked.

"Eris is punishing the people of Oceania," Zuma said sadly.

Merliah narrowed her eyes, determined. "We'll stop her."

Just then the royal conch rang through the water, and Remo tossed anemones like fireworks. The giant jellyfish pulled Eris in her chariot. Manta shark guards surrounded her as she reached the crowd.

Eris peered down at her subjects. "I only grant my Merillia to those who prove their love and devotion," she began. "Oceana, do you adore me?"

The crowd cheered wildly, but it wasn't good enough for Eris. Her face darkened.

"I don't believe you!" she yelled. "If you truly adored me, one of you would give me information about Calissa's daughter!"

Silence.

"Mantas, get me an answer!"

The merfolk in the crowd all cried out in despair as the manta sharks closed in.

"Wait!"

Merliah swam forward. With her fake tail, no one could tell that she wasn't a mermaid.

Eris glared down at her. "Do you have information about Calissa's daughter?"

"No, I don't," Merliah replied.

Eris's temper flared. "And yet you dare speak to me?" She raised her arm to create one of her wicked whirlpools.

"Please, wait!" Merliah cried. "I may not have that information, but I do have a gift

to prove our love and devotion." Kayla and Xylie swam up beside her. "I think you'll like it very much."

Eris arched her eyebrow. "I'd better."

Merliah, Kayla, and Xylie all gulped.

Snouts swam into view with the Deep-Sea-3 Player in his fins. A catchy and familiar tune blasted through the water.

She's the Queen of the Waves.
Check it out—she's spinnin' that pool around.
Queen of the Waves.
No one's gonna take away her crown.
(Her Majesty'll knock 'em dead.)
Surf's up! Bow down.
She's the Queen of the Waves!

It was the song Fallon and Hadley always played for Merliah at surf meets, slightly

altered for Eris!

As the mermaids and Snouts started to dance, the tune was so catchy that the crowd couldn't help joining in. Some merfolk beat on shells like drums, while others shook sand-filled shells like maracas. Everyone started dancing.

In all the hubbub, Merliah danced closer to Eris. It was time to put her plan into action! Could she get close enough to grab

Eris's necklace?

Slowly, Merliah, Kayla, and Xylie danced closer and closer to Eris. She was having so much fun that she didn't even notice! With a final deep breath, Merliah swam right up and tore the necklace away.

The music screeched to a halt. The crowd froze. Merliah had completed all three tasks, but there was no exciting, magical transformation like she'd expected. Instead Eris, the manta sharks, and the whole crowd of merpeople were silent—and they were staring at her.

This meant trouble!

Merliah turned and darted through the water as fast as she could. She clutched the necklace in one hand.

"STOP HER!" Eris screeched in fury.

A manta shark lunged forward, grabbing the end of Merliah's tail. The fabric ripped and revealed her human legs! The crowd gasped, but Eris's gasp was loudest of all. As soon as she saw Merliah's legs, she knew that it was Calissa's daughter—the girl who could destroy her!

Eris's voice cut through the water. "YOU!"

The manta sharks surrounded Merliah

and her friends. There was no escape.

Eris swam up and hovered nose to nose with Merliah. "You dare try to vanquish me?" she cried, enraged. She spun her entire body around with amazing speed. A giant, churning whirlpool appeared in the water. A group of manta sharks held Kayla, Xylie, Zuma, and Snouts back while the other manta sharks pushed Merliah directly into the spinning whirlpool.

"This whirlpool will take her to the bottom of the deepest trench in the ocean, where she'll never be heard from again!" Eris announced. The crowd was silent. "What, no applause?" the wicked queen roared.

The merfolk cheered weakly.

Inside the whirlpool, Merliah was slammed from side to side. She was losing all hope—until she remembered the dreamfish.

"Dreamfish, I need you!" she called.

The next instant, the dreamfish appeared and the interior of the whirlpool around Merliah calmed.

"I will offer you your greatest desire," he said, smiling. "I will send you back home to Malibu, and your mermaid half will go away. It will be like none of this ever happened."

Merliah was stunned. "You can do that?"

"It's your greatest desire," the dreamfish answered simply.

"But all this trouble in Oceana will still be happening, right?" Merliah said. "I just

won't be a part of it."

"Will you accept the wish?" the dreamfish asked.

Merliah paused. "No. Whatever else I am, I am Merliah, half-mermaid princess of Oceana. I must protect my subjects."

At her words, the whirlpool filled with strange bubbles. Before she knew it, the dreamfish had vanished and Merliah was completely surrounded by the bubbles.

When the water cleared again, Merliah looked around in wonder. It didn't take long to see what had changed. She had a beautiful tail—and this one was real!

Merliah smiled, swishing her tail back and forth. It was awfully strong. . . .

Back in the center of Oceana, Eris was still basking in the glow of banishing Merliah.

But that didn't last long.

With a swish of her powerful tail, Merliah leaped right out of the whirlpool! The crowd gasped. No one had escaped one of Eris's whirlpools before!

Eris gawked at Merliah, then turned to her manta sharks. "GET HER!"

The manta sharks surrounded Merliah, but she stood tall and spoke powerfully. "You don't have to take orders from Eris. She's not the rightful heir—I am, and I can

prove it. I have the Celestial Comb!" She pulled the comb from her hair as the crowd watched in wonder.

"Never mind that," Eris scoffed. "She's half-human! She can't spin Merillia! If you want the sea to survive, you need me and my precious Merillia."

Merliah's eyes lit up. "You don't need Eris to spin Merillia. Look!" She smashed Eris's necklace against a nearby rock, and the Merillia from inside spun through the water. Suddenly, everyone could see the image of Calissa in the dungeon.

"Is that really her?" merfolk in the crowd whispered. "Queen Calissa?"

Merliah whirled to face Eris, suddenly understanding. "You needed my mother to spin Merillia—because you can't. You're different, and you hate it."

Eris couldn't control her temper any longer. "LIAR! SEIZE HER!"

But no one did.

Merliah went on. "You've been pretending that my mother's Merillia is yours. But Calissa isn't happy, and that's why her Merillia is weak."

Eris couldn't take it any longer. "NOOOOO!" she screamed. She lunged at Merliah, filled with rage. But Merliah ducked out of the way . . . and Eris tumbled into her own powerful whirlpool! Within seconds, the wicked queen had disappeared, headed to the deepest trench in the ocean by her own horrible magic.

Oceana was filled with a shocked silence.

After a moment, the merfolk began to applaud, louder and louder. Even the manta

sharks bowed to Merliah.

"I'm not your queen," Merliah said, pointing to the image of Calissa still floating in the water. "She is. We need to find her."

Remo piped up, looking guilty. "I know where she is."

Chapter 10

Moments later, Merliah stood in the doorway to Calissa's dungeon cell, with all her friends behind her. "Mom?" she said softly.

Calissa turned from spinning Merillia. "Merliah?" She could hardly believe it. She zoomed to her daughter, wrapping her in a tight hug. "You're here! And you've grown a tail! Where's Eris?"

"We don't have to worry about Eris anymore. You're free! Oceana belongs to you again." Merliah smiled at her mother.

Snouts swam up with the royal crown perched on his head. Merliah handed it to her mother. "I'll tell you everything," Merliah promised. "But first I think we need to empty out Eris's dungeons."

The next day, the people of Oceana—including the released prisoners—gathered in the city center to celebrate Merliah's victory and Calissa's return. Calissa's subjects were returned to their families. And best of all, the coral throughout Oceana was lush, healthy, and beautiful again.

"It's wonderful to see the two of you together," said Zuma, beaming at Merliah and her mother.

"With a tail, you can stay with us forever!" Xylie squealed, hugging Merliah.

Merliah couldn't help smiling sadly.

Calissa noticed the wistful look on her daughter's face. "But there are things you would miss."

Merliah nodded. "I love all of you. But I'm sad that I'll never see Malibu again, or Fallon and Hadley, or Grandpa. I'll miss being human." She looked away.

Calissa lifted Merliah's chin. "You will always be human, and you will always be a mermaid. You are both. All you have to be is yourself."

At that, Calissa's three magical shells spun up into the water, and strands of silver Merillia began to form. "My friends?" she called.

In no time, all three Destinies approached on their sea horses and plucked a hair from Merliah's head. They set the hair afloat in the water in front of Calissa. Then a beautiful clamshell and the Merillia that Calissa had just spun floated over to join it. As Calissa worked her magic, the hair and Merillia wove together to form a chain. Then Calissa added the shell to the necklace as well. When she was finished, the necklace floated over to Merliah and settled around her neck. It was beautiful!

Merliah studied it and turned to her mother. "It's different from the one you gave me when I was a baby."

Calissa nodded. "This necklace is even more special. It's made from Merillia *and* your own hair. When you wish on it, you can control how you appear—human or mermaid. That way, you can return to the human world, and you can visit the mermaid

world whenever you like. You are unique, you are special, and that's what makes you strong."

Merliah hugged her mother with tears in her eyes. "Thank you!" She hesitated. "Would it be okay if I went home now? I just know Grandpa's worried about me."

Calissa smiled. "Come back soon and visit."

"I will," Merliah said, beaming at her mother and her new friends. She knew now that she wasn't a misfit at all—in fact, she had two homes where she fit perfectly. "I promise."

Epilogue

A few days later, Merliah was back in the water, tearing up the waves on her surfboard. Fallon and Hadley cheered her on from the beach.

She's the Queen of the Waves.
Check it out—she's spinnin' that board around.
She's the Queen of the Waves.
No one's gonna take away her crown.
(Her Majesty is dropping in.)
Surf's up! Bow down.
She's the Queen of the Waves!

Merliah grinned, tossing her pink hair out of her eyes. At the end of her run, she shot out of the tube perfectly. No wipeout this time—it was a perfect score!

As the crowd on the beach roared their approval, Merliah flipped off her board and into the water. Nearby, she could see Kayla, Xylie, Zuma, Snouts, and Calissa all cheering for her. She waved and blew them a kiss before swimming back to the shore.

Merliah couldn't help grinning. She

knew she was different. But she also knew that she didn't have to decide between being a surfer girl or a mermaid princess. She could be both. And together, those two parts made her better than ever!